My Forever Home

WWW.LOVE2READ2YOU.COM
Copyright © 2022 'MY FOREVER HOME'
ISBN: 9781706079620 (Amazon Paperback)
ISBN: 978-988-79833-1-6 (MJL Paperback).
Published in Hong Kong by Melissa Jane Lavi

My Forever Home

Dedicated to
Adele and Ethan
for being the inspiration
and collaborators
for this story.

"What does it mean
to be adopted?"

"Well, some babies come out of their Mummy's tummy and some babies do not.
Those who do not, are often adopted.

JUST LIKE ME!"

"But just like you,
I am part of a loving family."

"My Mummy and Daddy wanted a baby so much, but my Mummy's tummy couldn't make a baby of her own."

"Luckily someone else's could.
Someone who wasn't ready
to have her own baby yet.

When we were matched
my Mummy cried tears of happiness
and my Daddy jumped up and
down for joy."

"The moment that they saw me
they knew that I was their baby.
After all, they had carried
me in their hearts in the
same way that your Mummy
carried you in her tummy."

978-988-79833-1-6

"The reason that I look different from my family is because I come from a place far away, and I have the features of my birth father and my birth mother who carried me in her tummy."

"I have many questions about my adoption and my parents try to help me understand as much as they can. And I love learning about the place where I was born and I am very proud of that special part of who I am."

"I do this together with
my whole family, because it is
also a part of who they are now."

"So it really doesn't
matter if you come from
your Mummy's heart
or your Mummy's tummy.

Being part of a loving family
is a great place to be."

JUST LIKE ME!

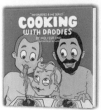    

Made in United States
Troutdale, OR
12/28/2024

27385482R00017